Praise for
Shivers, Scares, and Goosebumps
and Vonnie Winslow Crist

"Vonnie Winslow Crist's tales are precisely aimed at pre- and early teens for late night reads before bed, sleepovers, or campouts, and wow, do they hit the mark. These tales are a superb bridge between fairy tales and mainstream speculative fiction, written for youngsters with vivid imaginations who love to be frightened. *Shivers, Scares, and Goosebumps* should be on the shelves of every cool parent or grandparent, I certainly wish it was when I was a young boy. Will I be reading these stories to my grandchildren? You bet I will!"

~ Tony Tremblay,
Author of *The Moore House* and *Do Not Weep For Me*

"I loved this book! If you're looking for a story to tell around the campfire on a moonlit night, your search is over. In *Shivers, Scares, and Goosebumps*, Vonnie Winslow Crist masterfully weaves words into spooky tales that you'll remember and want to share, again and again. After reading *Shivers, Scares, and Goosebumps*, you'll have second thoughts about carving that Halloween pumpkin. You'll shiver when waiting for the tooth fairy to come, and goosebumps will rise like chicken pox at the thought of finding a mudpuppy. Read it alone in the dead of night but remember to check under the bed before you start."

~ Lois Szymanski,
Author of dozens of books for young readers,
including *The Gettysburg Ghost Gang*,
co-written by Shelley Sykes.

"Shivers, Scares, and Goosebumps is a wonderful collection! I haven't been a young reader since Gerald Ford was president and I loved this book. Writing non-dumbed down horror for younger readers is hard. And yet, Vonnie Winslow Crist makes is look effortless. I mean it as the highest compliment when I say that her stories would be right at home in an early 1970s Scholastic Book Club horror anthology. Plus, Vonnie's illustrations perfectly compliment the stories and manage to take an amazing collection to even higher levels of enjoyment."

~ Douglas Draa, Editor of *Weirdbook Magazine*

"Do you dare to be a little bit scared? Come along, it will happen, and it won't be just a little bit! A plethora of wondrously illustrated stories awaits, challenging you all the way to their endings—and beyond. I loved them all. I enjoyed *Shivers, Scares, and Goosebumps* so much, I read it in one day! The black and white renderings are simply brilliant! I am sure the child who gets this book will treasure it—especially when it's time to turn off the lights and tell scary stories. Of course, you need a little kid beside you for the 'GOT YOU' parts! Crist's poems were a treat and enhance the reading. Poetry should be in every child's reading library. I loved that she included folklore and stories inspired by tales from other countries. Not to mention, of course, her own 'real' stories, too."

~ Marge Simon,
Bram Stoker Award winning author
of *Vampires, Zombies & Wanton Souls*

"Vonnie Winslow Crist is a chameleon of a writer—as a reader, you never know where her tales will take you—yet there's always one thing you can count on: top-notch storytelling."

~ Richard Chizmar,
New York Times bestselling author of the Gwendy's Button
Box Trilogy and *The Girl on the Porch*

"As a writer, editor, and artist, Vonnie is a gem of our science fiction-fantasy community."

~ Tom M. Doyle,
award-winning author of the American Craft series,
Border Crosser, and *The Wizard of Macatawa*

Shivers, Scares, and Goosebumps

Written and Illustrated by
Vonnie Winslow Crist

From
Dark Owl Publishing, LLC

Arizona

The following stories are reprinted by permission of the author. The author thanks the editors and publishers where these stories appeared in an earlier form.

"Mudpuppy" ©2020, originally published in *Waters of Destruction*, 2020.
"Under Toad" ©2019, originally published in *Mother Ghost's Grimm, Volume 1*, 2019.
"Saying Goodbye" ©2019, originally published in *Beyond: A Dark Drabbles Anthology*, 2019.
"One Easter" ©2020, originally published in *Scary Snippets: Easter Edition*, 2020.
"Visiting" ©2019, originally published in *Beyond: A Dark Drabbles Anthology*, 2019.
"Fatted Squash" ©2019, originally published in *Scary Snippets: Halloween Edition*, 2019.
"Strays" ©2020, originally published in *Halloween Frights & Autumn Delights*, 2020.
"Wren Boys" ©2019, originally published in *Scary Snippets: Christmas Edition*, 2019.
"Mitten Tree" ©2019, originally published in *Scary Snippets: Christmas Edition*, 2019.
"Ogerhunches" ©2020, originally published in *Mother Ghost's Grimm, Volume 2*, 2020.
"Night Raven" ©2020, originally published in *Winds of Despair*, 2020.

Books by Vonnie Winslow Crist

The Chronicles of Lifthrasir
The Enchanted Dagger
Beyond the Sheercliffs

Novelette
Murder on Marawa Prime

Story Collections
By Scant Moonlight
Other Skies Above
Dragon Rain
Beneath Raven's Wing
Owl Light
The Greener Forest

Young Adult and Middle Grade
Shivers, Scares, and Goosebumps

Children's
Leprechaun Cake & Other Tales

Poetry Collections
River of Stars
Essential Fables

More Young Readers Books from Dark Owl Publishing

Grayson North
Frost Keeper of the Windy City
A totally cool urban fantasy adventure
by Kevin M. Folliard

Annette: A Big, Hairy Mom
A touching story of a boy and
his motherly friend, a Sasquatch
both written and illustrated by John S. McFarland

In addition, all books from Dark Owl Publishing are
appropriate for at least teenagers to read.

Please see the Young Readers Bookstore page
on our website
for details on age appropriateness.

www.darkowlpublishing.com/the-yr-bookstore

For Ernie,
Tim and Dawn,
Phil, Kristin, Nathaniel and Gabriel,
Melissa and Aria,
And all those who enjoy
Shivery, scary, goosebump-filled tales.

Table of Contents

Mudpuppy

In March, Brandie pulled on her waterproof boots.

"I'm going for a walk by the stream. See you later," she told her mother.

"Be careful not to fall in the water. It's still freezing," said Mom.

"Don't worry," replied Brandie. She slammed out the door and raced down their driveway. After crossing Creek Road, she climbed down to a grassy trail that wound through the trees a few yards from Rock Run.

Rock Run traveled beside the road for several miles before veering off and snaking through the woods. Unless a parent was with her, Brandie only hiked along the path for about a quarter mile. In that quarter mile, there were several driveways leading to neighbors' homes and the forest wasn't too thick.

Nearby, Rock Run gurgled as it tumbled between rocks and over fallen logs. Brandie knew it was too early for catching frogs, but she still looked at the banks of the stream, hoping to spot a turtle.

As she crossed over a culvert, Brandie noticed something squirming beside the stream. She climbed down from the trail to see what it was.

The creature had the shiny skin of an amphibian. It was brown with a few spots along its sides. Two black-as-night eyes peered at Brandie from the creature's head. She noticed its snout was rounded with nostril slits near the end.

"Are you a mudpuppy?" she asked the long-bodied

amphibian. Brandie remembered reading about stream animals in a book she had borrowed from the library.

The salamander-like animal squeaked. It moved its feet and tail.

"Are you stuck on land?" Brandie asked. She was worried the poor mudpuppy's skin would dry out if it didn't get back into the water soon.

The mudpuppy squeaked again.

"I'll help you," she promised. Then, she looked around for something with which to pick up the creature. She saw no large leaves or wide patches of moss. Concerned she might injure the mudpuppy if she used a branch or piece of bark, Brandie gently picked up the animal with her hands.

Without warning, the mudpuppy bit her finger.

She yelped as much from surprise as from pain.

"Let go," said Brandie as she tried to pry open the amphibian's mouth.

The mudpuppy shook its head.

"You are hurting me." Tears leaked from the corners of Brandie's eyes. Her finger was throbbing.

The mudpuppy refused to release its grip.

Brandie was afraid the creature would bite off part of her finger. She looked around for something to help remove the amphibian. She spotted a stick just a few steps downstream and hurried to it. As she bent to pick up the stick, her foot slipped on a mossy rock.

"Oh, no!" shouted Brandie. She fell into the icy water with a splash.

Rather than release its hold, the strong-jawed mudpuppy bit down harder. Within seconds, dozens of mudpuppies squirmed from their burrows. They swam to Brandie and grabbed the skin of her arms, legs, and hands with their mouths. Soon, all that could be seen in Rock Run was a pile of wriggling, chewing mudpuppies.

When Brandie didn't come home later that day, her parents called the police. The police looked for Brandie for hours. All they found were her bare, white bones. Something had licked her skeleton clean of flesh.

"What animal could have done such a thing?" asked an officer as she studied the water gurgling over the stream's rocks.

"I can't imagine," replied another police officer. "But whatever it was, I don't want to meet it."

Clean Your Room

Drew hated chores.

When his mother asked Drew to take out the trash and recyclables, he would say he was working on his homework. Which was usually untrue. When his father asked him to help rake leaves, Drew would say he was preparing a presentation for school. Which was almost always a lie. When his grandmother asked him to fill the dog's water bowl, he would tell her he had just washed his hands for dinner. Which was usually false.

Whether unloading the dishwasher, carrying in groceries, or cleaning his room, Drew didn't want to help. In fact, his room had gotten so messy, his father threatened to gather everything up and place it in garbage bags for Drew to sort through in the basement.

The only thing Drew hated more than chores was their basement. The basement was cold, poorly lit, rarely used, and smelled strange. So, with much grumbling, he went to his room with a trash bag in one hand and the laundry basket in the other hand.

Drew tossed trash into the bag and dirty clothes into the basket. As he worked, he heard scratching.

Maybe Mom is right, and a mouse has come to live in my room, he thought.

"I'm going to set a trap for you if you don't leave," he threatened.

The scratching stopped.

Drew picked up books and toys that had been scattered around his bedroom. As he picked them up, he heard scraping sounds.

Those noises are too big for a mouse, he thought. *Mom called my bedroom a rat's nest, so maybe a rat lives in here.*

He shuddered. He wasn't afraid of a mouse, but a rat was much bigger. Plus, it had bigger teeth.

"I can set a bigger trap if I need to," he said bravely. Even though Drew did not feel courageous.

Drew finished tidying most of his room. The only places left to clean were the closet and under his bed. The closet had a light in it, but Drew had to step inside while it was still dark to reach the light's pull-chain. He decided to save the closet for last.

Standing beside his bed, he saw dirty socks, balls of wadded paper, one of his old shoes, the arm of a navy blue sweater, pajama bottoms, pencils, straws, dust, and other stuff poking out. Before he could begin pulling things out from under his bed, Drew heard a growl.

He stepped back. Drew knew mice didn't growl. He supposed rats didn't growl either.

"I don't know what you are," said Drew as he grabbed an eighteen-inch ruler from the top of his desk and held it like a sword. "But I can find a trap big enough for you."

The growling stopped.

Legs shaking, Drew used a broom to drag out the socks and shoe.

He heard scratching.

Heart racing, Drew used the broom's handle to sweep out the paper wads, straws, and pencils.

He heard scraping.

Hairs on the back of his neck standing up, Drew knelt to gather the dirty sweater, pajama bottoms, and other clothes.

He heard growling. Suddenly, a head popped out.

Drew held the ruler in front of him as he stared into the yellow eyes of a green-skinned goblin. The hideous creature had wild hair and a row of sharp teeth.

"Is your trap big enough for me?" asked the goblin before

6

it stretched its claws toward Drew.

"No," stuttered Drew. "And sorry. I didn't mean to threaten you. I didn't know you were living under my bed."

"Goblins only live in dark, smelly, untouched places. Under your bed is warmer than the basement, so I moved in." The goblin smiled.

Drew counted even more teeth.

"Now that you have discovered me, I must rejoin my family in the basement," said the goblin as he scrambled out from beneath Drew's bed. "But I won't be going alone."

"Wait!" exclaimed Drew.

"Nope!" said the goblin as he grabbed Drew. Before Drew could call out for help, the goblin whisked him out of his bedroom, down the hall, and through the basement door.

"Now, don't you wish you had cleaned your room sooner?" asked the goblin.

Drew nodded, but was too frightened to scream. For one by one, the goblin's kinfolk stepped from the shadows. Each member of the goblin troop held a knife and fork.

"I see you brought us dinner," growled the biggest goblin. She lunged for Drew. "GOTCHA!" she said as she wrapped her lime-green, goblin fingers around Drew's arm.* "Bring me my stew pot," she ordered. "And sharpen my biggest knife."

*If you are reading this story to someone else, you can grab their arm when you say this.

Lunar Phase

full moon
magical light
streaming between birch trees
summoning the darkness within

wolf moon
a howled warning before the hunt
swallowing screams, prey flees
nowhere to hide

blood moon

Ghost Pack

"**W**hy does Uncle Amos feed other people's dogs and strays?" Ollie Pomfret asked his mom. He watched their neighbor scrape his dinner leftovers into a bowl.

Ollie knew the food was for the beagle from down the street. The beagle came every day to Uncle Amos's house to eat because the family who owned the hound often forgot to take care of him.

"He is kind," Mom answered. "I wish more people were like him."

Ollie nodded. Then, before running over to Uncle Amos's house, he called, "I'll be home by eight."

"No later," said his mother.

***

"Hi." Ollie sat beside his neighbor on Uncle Amos's garden bench.

"Good evening," replied Uncle Amos. He was scratching the hound's neck.

Ollie bent down. He scratched the beagle, too. Then, he glanced at the old man whom everyone in the neighborhood called Uncle Amos. "How many dogs have you adopted, taken care of until they died, and buried in your yard?"

"Thirteen, so far," said Uncle Amos. He tilted his head toward the backyard.

"Wow! You must really love dogs!" exclaimed Ollie.

"I do," replied his neighbor as he patted the grateful beagle.

***

That night, Ollie woke to red and blue lights flashing and sirens wailing. He ran downstairs, then out onto the porch where Mom already stood.

"What happened?" he asked.

He shivered as he watched a stretcher carrying a body bag roll out of Uncle Amos's house.

"Someone killed Uncle Amos," said Mom. She wiped her eyes with a tissue. "I cannot imagine why anybody would harm such a gentle soul."

Ollie spotted paramedics wheeling a second stretcher out of the house. It, too, appeared to have a plastic-wrapped body on it.

"Who is that?" he asked.

"The police don't know," answered Mom. "Whomever it was, they were torn to shreds by animals. Probably coyotes."

"No," whispered Ollie. "There aren't that many coyotes around here." He studied their neighbor's backyard for a moment. "But there *are* plenty of dogs who loved Uncle Amos."

His mother frowned at him. "I have no idea what you are talking about. Now, go back to bed."

Before he climbed the stairs to his bedroom, Ollie saw all thirteen dog graves in Uncle Amos's yard had been disturbed. He was sure the graves hadn't been dug open from above with a shovel, but from below with skeletal paws. And he was just as certain the ghosts of the dogs Uncle Amos had rescued rushed to help their friend. Though they couldn't save Uncle Amos, the ghost dogs had finished off his attacker.

***

Every night after the night of Uncle Amos's murder, Ollie heard soft howls and dog toenails clicking outside his window. He knew it was Uncle Amos's ghost pack digging out of their graves, racing up driveways, through yards, across streets, and under the trees in the woods behind Ollie's house.

He suspected the pack was hunting for other cruel people. He also believed when the skeleton dogs caught the evil doers, they tore them apart.

Ollie repeated the story of Uncle Amos's undead dogs to his friends, who told their friends, who told their friends. Soon, everyone in the county knew to lock their doors if they heard faint howling and the pad of dogs' feet after sundown. Then, starting the next morning, to be kinder to animals.

To this day, Ollie Pomfret warns anyone who will listen: When the wind sighs and the moon glows, if you hear toenails clicking or bony paws rustling leaves—beware. It's the ghost pack on the prowl.

And they might be looking for YOU!*

*When you read this line, point at one of the listeners.

Under Toad

Standing on the shore, Sheila bent over every now and again to pick up a seashell. When she spotted a wave rushing toward her, she squealed. Then she ran from the foam so quickly her toes were barely wet.

"Come in the water," called her brother, Bret. He was in the ocean up to his waist.

"No, thanks." Sheila didn't want to add she was afraid of the under toad.

"The surf is calm. It won't knock you over," shouted her brother as a gentle swell washed past him.

Sheila looked at her mom and dad sitting on the beach beneath an umbrella in striped folding chairs. If the under toad grabbed her, they should be able to save her in time.

"Okay," she said. Setting her bucket of shells safely above the tide line, she walked into the saltwater.

She felt her toes sinking into the sand as the seawater swept in and out. Looking up, Sheila spotted gulls floating on the late afternoon winds. Their bird cries were so loud she heard them over the slosh of the surf.

"You are right, this *is* fun," she told her brother.

"Why didn't you come in earlier?" Bret asked as a cresting wave splashed his face.

"I remember Aunt Edna warning me to be careful of the under toad. It is a terrible creature which sleeps at the edge of the ocean," said Sheila.

Her older brother laughed. "It's undertow, not under toad.

You don't really think there is a big amphibian lurking beneath the ripples?" He laughed again.

"Aunt Edna told me the under toad pulls careless children out into the deeper water. Then, it drowns them," replied Sheila. Just saying the words out loud made her shiver.

Bret laughed so hard he snorted.

Sheila felt silly until she saw two large, webbed, warty hands reach up from the ocean. The frog-like hands wrapped around Bret's arm and yanked him below the surface.

"Mom! Dad!" Sheila screamed as she raced from the ocean. "The under toad has Bret."

At first, her parents laughed. But when they saw the fear in Sheila's eyes was real, they stopped laughing. They jumped up from their striped chairs and raced into the surf to look for her brother.

The lifeguards looked, too. Next, the police and volunteers tried to locate Bret. Her parents and the other people searching did not laugh hours later when the moon rose and her brother was still missing.

Sheila knew the under toad had Bret, even if no one else but Aunt Edna believed her.

Under Toad

Saying Goodbye

D ressed in jeans, sweater, and fringed boots, a teenager
stood in The Little Bakery's doorway.

For a second, Ella didn't say anything. She just
stared.

The teen was a dead ringer for her cousin, Toni. But she
knew it couldn't be Toni, because she was already on her
way to their grandmother's house for Thanksgiving. Ella
and her mother wouldn't be leaving until later this
afternoon after the shop closed. So, Toni had decided to drive
herself.

"Can I help you?" asked Ella. "The bakery doesn't open for
another fifteen minutes, but you are welcome to sit and
wait." Ella pointed to six cafe tables and chairs at the front
of the shop.

The girl tapped her chest. She hugged herself. Then, she
took a step forward with her arms outstretched.

Maybe she's having a heart attack, thought Ella. She
grabbed her phone from a pocket. She hated coming in early
to Mom's bakery to turn on the coffee and set things up.
Sure, it helped her mother out, but it was creepy being in
the shop by herself.

"Do you need help?" Ella asked.

Toni's double smiled faintly. She shook her head.

Suddenly, Ella's phone rang. She was so surprised, she
nearly dropped the device. After taking a deep breath, Ella
answered.

"Is someone else there with you?" asked her mother. "Maybe Betty or one of the other bakers?"

"Why?" Ella couldn't imagine what news Mom was going to tell her that required other people to be present.

"Because what I'm going to say is very upsetting," replied her mother. "I wanted to call and tell you before you heard it on the television."

"Well, I'm here alone except for an early customer." Ella smiled at the teenager that looked like her cousin. The girl smiled back and sat in a chair at the table nearest the door. "And I haven't turned on the television yet."

"I don't know how else to say this than to be direct," began Mom. "There was an accident on the interstate. The police have not shared the details yet, but Toni was killed."

Phone still against her ear, Ella turned around. Toni's ghost pressed her hand against her chest once more, smiled, then vanished.

"Toni was just here," whispered Ella. "She came to say goodbye."

"Impossible," gasped Mom.

But Ella knew it was true.

Trophies

RJ studied the landscape whizzing by the car windows as his father drove to Buck Lake. He was not looking forward to the annual Grier Family Campout. Sure, there were relatives he liked seeing, good food to be eaten, and trails to be hiked, but Cousin Boots would be there.

Cousin Boots was a hunter. Or at least he claimed to be one. More than one Grier relation had hinted that most of the trophies decorating Boots's cabin had been purchased from the local taxidermist. Cousin Boots always protested loudly. Then, he would launch into a hunting tale.

To prove the accuracy of his aim and his unfailing ability to find game, Boots described in great detail every hunt he had been on. As further proof of his skills and the truthfulness of his stories, he filled his cabin with labeled trophies. Trophies he happily showed RJ, his parents, and sisters.

Unfortunately, the Grier Family Campout was held at the Buck Lake Campgrounds, which adjoined Cousin Boots's property. Family members with campers and tents stayed at the campgrounds. Since RJ's family did not own either, they stayed with Cousin Boots. Mom and Dad stayed in one spare room. RJ's sisters, Pam and Zoey, stayed in the other spare bedroom. Which left RJ the sofa in the living room for a bed.

But RJ had trouble sleeping in the living room. Not only were the heads of Cousin Boots's conquered game animals displayed on every spare inch of the walls, but various hides were draped on chairs, tables, and the sofa back. Luckily, Cousin Boots gave RJ a plaid blanket at bedtime. No matter how chilly the night, RJ would have huddled beside the fireplace rather than wrap himself in animal skins.

"We are here!" exclaimed RJ's father. "And it's not bedtime yet."

"Hooray! Finally!" squealed Pam and Zoey.

"Great," mumbled RJ.

Everyone grabbed their suitcases and hurried to Cousin Boots's cabin, except RJ. He walked slowly. If he could delay going inside the cabin for even a few minutes, he chose to do so. It made his skin crawl to see the fake eyes in the animals' eye sockets. Though the deer, bears, goats, elk, moose, bobcat, mountain lion, lynx, and other mounted heads appeared almost alive, RJ knew they were dead. And deep in his bones, he knew their spirits were not at peace. How could they be, with their heads displayed on Cousin Boots's walls?

"Come on in, RJ," said his cousin. Boots grabbed RJ's shoulder and pulled him inside. "Don't be a laggard. I've got a new trophy to show you."

"Great," replied RJ. He kept his eyes on the floor. He didn't want to look any of the dead animals in their glass eyes.

"What do you think?" Cousin Boots gave RJ a little shove. "Got myself a piebald buck."

Dreading the sight, nevertheless RJ lifted his eyes to gaze at the deer. It was brown with white markings, or maybe, it was white with brown markings. It was hard to determine which.

"Used its legs, too, to make a new lamp," said his cousin.

RJ glanced at the nearest end table. Sure enough, there were four deer legs lashed together around the lamp's center post. Lower down, four hooves pointing in four different directions were attached to the lamp base. The tops of the legs were hidden by the deerskin lampshade.

"Impressive," he managed to say.

"I would say it is impressive," said Cousin Boots. "Only

one in every hundred whitetails is a piebald. Maybe less. So, I got me a rare find."

RJ was rescued from responding to his cousin when Dad asked, "Are we roasting marshmallows tonight?"

"Yup," said Cousin Boots. "Rest of the family is already over by the firepit."

***

It was nearly midnight when, full of marshmallows, chocolate, and graham crackers, they returned to the cabin. Exhausted from the long drive, RJ's parents and sisters went to their bedrooms immediately. Cousin Boots grabbed a drink from the refrigerator, then retired to his upstairs room as well. RJ could hear his cousin's television blaring, though he suspected Boots had fallen asleep.

With the living room lit only by the fire in the fireplace, RJ laid on the sofa beneath the plaid blanket. He glanced around the room. Stuffed raccoons, squirrels, skunks, groundhogs, beavers, muskrats, chipmunks, moles, and assorted other small mammals posed in almost natural positions. Plus, there was a flock of stuffed gamebirds as well. They seemed ready to scurry or fly back to the forest.

The firelight reflected from the animals' eyes with a sinister light. RJ found it hard to swallow. Something felt different about tonight. Usually, the Grier Family Campout was held close to July Fourth. This year, the Griers had decided to camp together at Midsummer. In fact, tonight was not only Midsummer's Eve, but a full moon as well.

The wall clock struck twelve. Rather than chime, each hour had a birdcall. For midnight, it was the hooting of an owl. Uneducated in owl song, RJ had no idea which owl called from the clock.

A sudden gust blew open the cabin's door.

Cousin Boots must not have locked the door, thought RJ.

From the corner of his eye, RJ saw movement. The preserved animals were stirring. A nearby raccoon shook its head. A wild turkey perched on a fake branch stretched its wing. Most frightening of all, the four deer legs tied to the lamp tapped their hooves.

Still wrapped in the blanket, RJ sat up. He didn't make a sound. Instead, he watched the not-quite-dead animals come alive. Those creatures that were still whole flew or crept away. As for the heads, one by one their skeletal bodies walked into the cabin. Once a head's skeleton was below it, the head dropped off the wall and reattached itself to the neck bones. If that animal's hide was draped over a piece of furniture, the skin crawled to its bones and flung itself over the skeleton. Then, the undead animal trotted out the door.

Finally, the lashings dropped away from the piebald deer's legs. A legless deer skeleton rolled into the cabin. Quick as a bullet, the legs joined with the rest of the bones and the white and brown deer head dropped to the neck bones. The piebald's hide crept down the stairs from Cousin Boots's room. It rejoined its skeleton. Lastly, the piebald studied RJ. It tilted its head, nodded its antlers, then bolted from the cabin.

RJ sat frozen in place for what seemed like an hour. Knees weak, he managed to stumble to the cabin door. He closed it, returned to the sofa, and sat staring at the fire. Sometime later in the night, he fell asleep.

***

When RJ awoke in the morning, he hoped last night had been a nightmare. He was wrong. All the stuffed animal trophies were gone. In their place, looking down from above the fireplace, was Cousin Boots's head mounted on a wooden trophy board.

RJ screamed and screamed for his parents.

Vampire

To soar in darkest night,
an undead leaves his grave
with a quick, black wing-flap.

He flies over the town
looking for a way in.
Beware—
Your window needs garlic.

One Easter

Christmas was Luvia's favorite holiday. Easter was her second favorite. She loved dressing up in her bright Easter witch clothes and visiting the houses in her village north of Helsinki. She always came home with a big bag of candy.

As a final touch to her witch disguise, Dad drew freckles on Luvia's cheeks.

"Have fun," said her father.

With a wave of her hand, Luvia ran out the door to join her best friend, Tetta. Along with dozens of other little witches, Tetta and she carried willow sticks.

"How much candy do you think we will get?" Tetta licked her lips.

"Probably the same as last year," replied Luvia. "I don't think anyone new has moved to the village."

Tetta shrugged her shoulders. "You are probably right. But let's hurry so we can visit as many houses as possible."

Luvia nodded. Then the best friends walked down their village's main street, knocking on doors.

When the residents opened their doors, Tetta and Luvia waved their willow branchlets. The sticks had been decorated with colorful paper streamers and feathers. Next, they handed a willow twig to each homeowner and chanted, "I wave a twig for a fresh and healthy year ahead. A twig for you. A treat for me!"

At every home, they were complimented on their costumes

and given sweets.

"My arm is tired," said Luvia. "I think we have collected enough candy." She lifted a cloth bag heavy with sweets. "Let's go home."

"Come on," urged Tetta. "We have another twig. Let's visit one last house."

Luvia sighed. She didn't want to upset her friend, so she accompanied Tetta to a cottage set far back off the road.

Tetta had knocked only once when the cottage's door swung open.

"Here to chase away the evil spirits?" asked an elderly man standing in the doorway. He motioned for them to come inside. "I have a basket of chocolate Easter eggs in the kitchen."

Luvia hesitated. Behind the man's home, she saw more than a dozen statues of children. The kids seemed to be running away. Some of them had terrible expressions on their faces.

"No, thanks. We are not supposed to go inside," said Luvia.

"Don't be a baby," said Tetta as she stepped into the cottage.

Luvia felt a chill creep up her spine. "We need to leave," she whispered.

Tetta laughed at her from inside the cottage.

Heart racing, Luvia dropped her last willow twig, turned, and ran. She heard Tetta cry out, but she didn't look back.

It must take more than a willow twig to banish truly evil spirits, thought Luvia. As she ran, Luvia heard footfalls behind her drawing closer.

She had almost reached the road when she felt a hand grasp her shoulder.

"GOT YOU!" said the old man.*

Luvia turned to stone so quickly that she couldn't even shout for help.

*If you are reading this story to someone else, you can grab their arm when you say this.

Vultures

Jimmie spotted three feral cats skulking along the edge of the woods. They were thin and ragged.

Feeling sorry for the strays, he put a scoop of dried cat food in an old bowl. Then, he set the bowl on the back porch. In the morning, the food was gone.

The next day, he set food out again. This time, after Jimmie went back inside, he sat by the window holding Lulu, his fluffy, white, indoor cat. Soon, three scrawny cats padded up the porch steps. They looked at Lulu and Jimmie watching from the window. The feral cats meowed, then gobbled up the food.

After feeding them for ten days, the strays trusted Jimmie enough to allow him to sit on the porch while they ate. Lulu sat inside, studying her wild cousins through the windowpane.

The following week, though she had said nothing at first, Jimmie's mom sighed loudly when he asked her to buy extra cat food for the feral cats.

"You shouldn't leave food out," his mother warned. "Every opossum, raccoon, and wood rat in the area will be stopping by our house for dinner."

"The strays eat the food before any other animals have a chance," said Jimmie.

"Maybe," replied Mom.

Jimmie thought she sounded unconvinced. Still, Mom bought the extra food.

Because his mother didn't tell him he *couldn't* feed the wild cats, Jimmie continued to put cat food out for the strays. In fact, now worried they might not get enough to eat if other animals took part of their meal, he put two bowls of food outside.

As spring turned to summer, every day the strays returned to Jimmie's porch and ate. Though they didn't allow him to pet them, the wild cats seemed almost tame. Jimmie even named the trio: Smokey was the gray cat; Ash was the black cat; and Flame was the orange one.

Soon, Smokey, Ash, and Flame sat by their bowls and groomed themselves after they had eaten. When the sunlight warmed the porch in the afternoon, they often curled up and took catnaps beneath the window.

One sultry day, Mom commented that there were no moles, chipmunks, squirrels, or mice digging in her garden this year. "I suppose it's those stray cats," she said. "I guess we will have to find a place for them to sleep in the shed before autumn."

Jimmie smiled. He knew Smokey, Ash, and Flame would love a warm bed in the shed to keep them dry in the cold fall rains and warm in the winter.

But the next morning, he discovered the cats weren't the only ones enjoying the porch. Five vultures were perched on the railing with their wings spread.

Although the bold carrion eaters' feathers shown like obsidian, Jimmie didn't like the looks in the vultures' eyes. They studied the cat food, cats, and Jimmie with such intensity, it made Jimmie's skin crawl.

He tried to shoo them away by yelling at the sharp-beaked birds from the open window. The vultures just squawked at him.

"They are warming their wings," explained his mother from the kitchen, "so they can fly."

Jimmie wasn't convinced. He suspected they were eating the food he put out for Smokey, Ash, and Flame.

"I'm going to the store for a few groceries. Do you want to come?" his mother asked. She picked up her car keys.

"No, I'll stay here," Jimmie answered.

"Fine," said Mom as she headed out the front door. "But no going outside until I get back."

"I will stay inside," he promised.

About five minutes later, Jimmie looked out the window at the vultures. One of them had jumped down from the railing. It was eating the food that belonged to Smokey, Ash, and Flame.

He opened the door and shouted, "No!"

The vulture didn't even look at him.

Angry at the bird, he forgot his promise, stepped out the back door, and onto the porch. He took two steps, then slipped and fell. He realized the vulture must have scattered some of the cat food pellets onto the porch's wooden floor.

Jimmie tried to sit up. He couldn't. His right leg and right shoulder hurt. The pain was so bad, it made Jimmie's stomach ache and his head spin.

He looked at the porch railing. The five vultures had returned. They hunched their shoulders and lowered their heads to get a better look at him. The meat-eating birds appeared to realize Jimmie couldn't move. He gazed at their sharp claws and hooked beaks.

Mom wouldn't be home for an hour. There was no one else around to hear him scream for help. If Smokey, Ash, and Flame didn't come and save him, Jimmie knew he was a goner.

Jimmie closed his eyes. He hoped to hear meowing, but he feared he would hear vultures landing on the porch beside him.

Visiting

Every summer, Granny and Mom wandered the cemetery checking the condition of the gravesites of relatives. Victoria hated to wander around the graveyard in the hot sun. So today, like usual, Victoria sat with Uncle Horton in the shade of an elm tree.

"I'm sorry it's been so long since I visited," she said as she held her great-uncle's hand.

Uncle Horton smiled.

"I know we only visit once a year when we come to Phelps," said Victoria. "I wish we could stop by more often."

Uncle Horton squeezed her hand.

"Would you like to hear about third grade?" she asked.

Her great-uncle nodded.

Victoria had expected him to nod. Uncle Horton always listened to her talk about the past school year, her friends, and dreams. Which is why she looked forward to their annual visit. Victoria had just begun chatting about her favorite book when her mother and grandmother waved to her.

"Time to leave," called Granny from the graveyard's entrance.

"Do we have to go?" asked Victoria. "I have barely gotten to talk with Uncle Horton."

"Don't be silly," scolded Granny. "Horton has been dead for twenty years. Now, come along."

Victoria looked at her great-uncle sitting beside her. He winked, then disappeared.

Tooth Fairy

The Tooth Fairy surveyed the toys scattered around Maria's room. If she questioned the stuffed donkey tucked beneath the blanket beside Maria, the girl would certainly wake up. The bear, piglet, bunny, kangaroo, tiger, or ragdoll perched on the windowsill were better choices. Having both of her button eyes and a clear view of the room, the fairy decided the doll was the toy to bring to life.

Raising her wand and whispering an awakening spell, the fairy tapped the ragdoll. The doll gasped. She shook her red yarn hair, then turned to look at the Tooth Fairy.

"I can talk!" exclaimed the ragdoll.

The fairy sighed. Newly animated toys always said the same thing. "Yes..." she replied, pausing for a moment to allow the doll to fill in her name.

"Annie," said the ragdoll. "I am Annie Striped-Socks."

"Well, Annie Striped-Socks, I need to ask you a few questions." The Tooth Fairy patted the skirt of her filmy dress.

"I will try to answer them." Annie rubbed her triangle nose with one of her hands.

"Has Maria been a good child since my last visit?" The Tooth Fairy had swapped a cuspid for several coins two months earlier. Every third tooth retrieval, she checked with a toy about a child's behavior. When next she spotted an elf or bunny, the fairy relayed the good and bad deeds of children. She knew her reports would get back to the North

Pole and Chief Rabbit. In order to keep up with the workload, magical beings often shared information.

Annie's embroidered eyebrows lowered and came together in a frown. "Maria has been good, but her brother, Jerry, has not. He snuck in after your last two visits. Quiet as the moon, he took some of the coins you left under Maria's pillow."

"He stole the tooth money!" The fairy angrily fluttered her wings. "No one gets coins from the Tooth Fairy unless I get their teeth."

Tapping her left palm with her wand, the fairy considered the appropriate punishment for stealing Maria's coins. "I will take two teeth from Jerry in exchange for the money he stole," she told Annie.

The doll nodded. "Fair is fair," she agreed. "Does Jerry have two loose teeth?"

"It doesn't matter," replied the Tooth Fairy. "I am owed two teeth."

"Oh, dear," said the ragdoll. Before she could comment further, the fairy chanted a sleep spell.

"Keep watch, Annie Striped-Socks," said the Tooth Fairy, "until I wake you again."

After sliding four shiny coins under Maria's pillow and kissing her brow, the fairy flew to her brother's bedroom.

The Tooth Fairy alighted on his pillow. She removed a pair of pliers from her tooth sack. Then, she whispered a spell to prevent Jerry from moving or crying out. With a smile on her lovely face, the fairy pushed open the boy's mouth.

"So many teeth," she mused as she studied his adult teeth. "Too bad you have to part with two for taking Tooth Fairy money from your sister."

By now, Jerry had opened his eyes and found he couldn't save himself from the fairy's revenge. The only thing he could do as the Tooth Fairy grasped one of his molars with her pliers and pulled was blink his eyes.

"These will make nice additions to my tooth castle," said the fairy as she slipped two of Jerry's teeth in her sack. "I suspect you will never take Tooth Fairy money again," she said. "But should you do so, I *will* return."

Before she vanished, the fairy tapped Jerry with her wand. Able to move once more, the boy sat up and screamed.

The Tooth Fairy's laughter filled his room. She knew his parents wouldn't believe Jerry when he told them what had happened to his missing teeth.

"Fair is fair," said the fairy as she headed for the next house on her list.

Last Farm

AZALEAS: LAST FARM AT THE END OF THE LANE proclaimed a faded sign.

Turning into the driveway, Lynn thought, *Mother's Day is tomorrow. I would love to have something to give to Mom.*

Two miles later, Lynn spotted rows and rows of azaleas blooming beside a tidy white farmhouse, tool shed, and garage. She parked her beat-up car, opened the door, and slid out. She studied the field of flowers.

"Howdy," said a man.

Lynn jumped. She hadn't seen the farmer when she pulled up. She wondered where he had come from. She decided he must have been in the tool shed, because he had a shovel in his hand.

"I saw your sign at the beginning of the lane," explained Lynn. "How much are the azaleas?" She prayed they were inexpensive. To be honest, Lynn had little money.

"Free!" replied the farmer. "I just want them to find a good home."

"That is amazing. They are so beautiful," said Lynn. "I will take one for my Mom, and I promise it will have a good home."

"One doesn't seem enough. How about four azaleas?" replied the farmer.

"I don't want to take too many," said Lynn. The man was being so generous. She didn't want to be greedy. "Other people might want some, too."

"Don't be silly." The farmer laughed. "There are plenty of plants for anyone who stops by."

"Okay. Four would be great." Lynn opened the trunk of her car. "Do you need me to help dig?"

"No, thanks," answered the farmer as he quickly dug one pink, one red, one white, and one purple azalea. "Here you go. I hope your mom enjoys the flowers." He smiled as he loaded four freshly-dug azaleas into her trunk.

Lynn closed the trunk, then turned to thank the man. She gasped. No one was there.

The farmhouse, tool shed, and garage that had looked like new a few minutes ago were now vine-covered ruins. She saw a rusted shovel leaning against a wooden FOR SALE sign in the middle of an overgrown lawn.

But the strangest thing of all was the field of azaleas had four fresh holes in the row of plants nearest the lane. It was clear someone had just dug four azaleas.

Lynn leaped into her car and hurried home. She didn't know what to tell her mother when she asked, "Where did you get these lovely azaleas?"

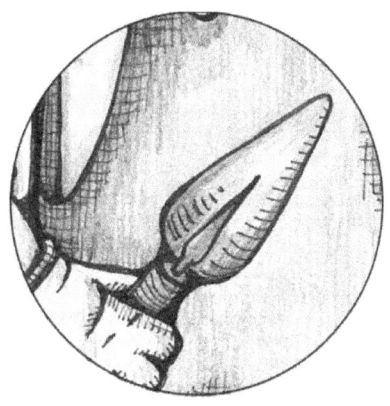

Whistle Past

alking by Kirkwood Cemetery, Dillion focused his eyes on the road ahead. He tried to push aside his fears by whistling past the graveyard. Without warning, a corpse-scented breeze drifted from the cemetery. The air smelled so awful, it made him cough.

"Argh!" he exclaimed as he covered his nose with his arm. "What is that stench?"

Dillion glanced to his right. Floating on the putrid wind was a beautiful, opal-eyed woman dressed in ebony robes.

His mouth would have dropped open from surprise if it hadn't been covered to prevent breathing the terrible smell. He gagged as the woman drew closer. The cloud she rode smelled like rotten meat.

"I am Kalma, Goddess of Death and Decay," said the woman "It is midnight. You should be home, fast asleep in your bed. You are *not* supposed to be here."

"Sorry," began Dillion. "I was playing a game at my friend's house. I didn't realize it had gotten so late." The stench was making him sick. He hoped he didn't throw up the snacks he had eaten earlier in the evening.

"Hush," whispered Kalma. She waved a bony hand before her.

From behind the Goddess of Death and Decay, Dillion saw spirits slipping from their graves. As he watched, dozens of ghosts joined Kalma. Then, the darksome throng vanished in an odoriferous whirlwind.

Ignoring the lingering stink, Dillion ran home. He promised himself to never walk past a cemetery at night again.

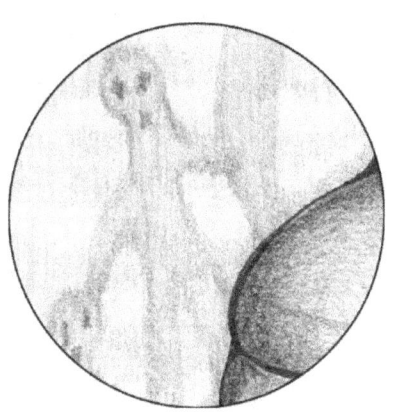

Aliens

Laura didn't mind babysitting the Campbell boys, but their dog drove her crazy. Andy, Pat, and Mikie would happily snack on popcorn and watch a movie on television. At nine o'clock, they would grumble when sent to bed, but listened. Usually, the boys were asleep within ten minutes. Then, Laura would watch the television until Mr. and Mrs. Campbell came home.

Tonight had been no different. Also no different was the behavior of the Campbell family's dog, Buster. Buster liked to bark, dig at the carpet, drag his dried dog food around the house, and chew on shoes. Buster liked to jump on the furniture, steal food, and only gave you a few seconds warning when he needed to go outside to relieve himself. Buster was the most annoying dog Laura knew.

Earlier in the evening, before too much damage was done, Laura had spotted Buster chewing on one of Andy's shoes. The left shoe would need new laces, but the gnawed edge of the tongue was barely noticeable. About an hour later, Buster had climbed onto the coffee table to steal some popcorn. His wagging tail had bumped the popcorn bowl. Luckily, Laura had grabbed the bowl before it spilled. Unfortunately, she hadn't caught the glass of water Buster had knocked over a few minutes later.

But all in all, tonight the little furball had been less annoying than usual.

She looked at Buster. He was standing by the front door.

A low grumble came from his throat. His nose was pressed to the floor. A glance at the doorknob told Laura the door was locked. Nonetheless, her heart skipped a beat when Buster suddenly began to bark.

His yapping grew louder and more urgent. The dog raced back to Laura, jumped on her lap, then hopped off and rushed to the door. He resumed barking. Every now and again, Buster stood on his hind legs and scratched on the door.

"What is it, boy?" she asked.

Buster stopped barking for a second. He looked over his shoulder at Laura. He whined several times before resuming his yapping.

Laura thought she heard noises outside. She picked up her phone and backed out of the living room towards the boys' bedrooms.

Rather than call the police, she phoned her parents. They lived two blocks away.

"Dad," said Laura when her father picked up. "I think there is someone in the Campbell's yard. Would you come over and check it out?"

"I'll be there in about five minutes," said her father. "Though I wouldn't get too excited. It is probably nothing."

No sooner had the word *nothing* been spoken, then the front door swung open.

Laura covered her mouth to stifle a scream. Three large aliens burst through the doorway. It was impossible to tell if the gaunt, gray creatures were there for good or evil. Their huge eyes, nostril slits, and wide mouths filled with jagged teeth showed no emotion.

Buster apparently believed the aliens were up to no good because he jumped at them. The little dog barked, growled, snapped his teeth, and clawed at the creatures. Laura knew he had no chance against three adversaries.

"What a brave pup," she whispered. Then, against her better judgment, she shouted, "Buster! Come."

She ran into Mikie's room, picked him up, and carried him into the bedroom Andy and Pat shared. Buster dashed into the room just before Laura closed the door. After flipping the lock, she pushed a chest of drawers in front of the door. Then she phoned the police.

Laura stood in the far corner of the bedroom. She pulled Andy, Pat, and Mikie close. She heard footsteps in the hallway. She saw the knob move.

Barking angrily, Buster raced toward the chest of drawers.

"What a brave pup," Laura whispered again.

Then, she held her breath and waited to see who or what would push through the door.

Scarecrow Dance

Sally stood at the edge of her grandparents' cornfield. The harvest moon rose round and gold over the drying corn. Its yellow light washed acres of corn, pumpkins, gourds, and acorn squash with an otherworldly glow.

Sally shivered. She usually thought her grandparents' farm looked warm and welcoming. It did not feel that way tonight.

A rustling sound caused Sally to look at the ground. Searching for kernels, several mice scampered between the cornstalks near the edge of the field. From a branch of the oak tree at the corner of the yard, a horned owl hooted. The large bird watched the mice with hungry interest.

A sudden gust of September wind caused stalks to rattle. But it was a different movement that caught Sally's eye. The scarecrow that hung in the center of the field began to dance.

"It's only the wind," she told herself. "Besides, he is far from me." But even saying those words didn't stop the coldness filling the pit of her stomach.

She continued to stare at the scarecrow as the breeze picked up. The strawman jigged enthusiastically. His movements didn't seem random. They appeared more like a real dance.

Sally's arms were now covered in goosebumps.

Even though she had to squint her eyes to make certain of what she was seeing, she swore the scarecrow had slipped off his wooden post. Instead of crumbling to the ground, he now wobbled around on his own. The scarecrow turned his head. He looked at Sally.

The back of Sally's neck prickled. It felt like every tiny hair there were standing straight out.

The scarecrow smiled. As he lumbered toward Sally, she was frozen in place.

"Go," she whispered. Her feet wouldn't obey. "Move," she said. Her legs wouldn't listen. "Run," she screamed. But she remained rooted in place.

The scarecrow arrived at the edge of the field. He stepped onto the lawn and reached for her hand.

"Sally, come dance in the moonlight," said the strawman in a voice as hollow as an empty skull.

"No!" She tried to pull her hand away from the gloved hand of the scarecrow, but she could not.

Once the strawman held her hand, Sally's feet began to dance. The scarecrow chuckled, then waltzed her back into the cornfield.

In the morning, Sally's grandparents found her. She was leaning on the wooden supports used for the corn field's scarecrow. Her lap was filled with sleeping field mice.

"Shoo!" exclaimed her grandfather as he waved a red handkerchief at the tiny rodents.

The mice scattered with a chorus of squeaks.

"What happened to your new shoes?" asked her grandmother. "They have holes worn in the bottoms of them."

"The scarecrow," replied Sally.

"What scarecrow?" said her grandfather. "The scarecrow is not here. Someone must have taken it."

Sally glanced up. The pole the scarecrow usually hung upon was empty. And though she couldn't be positive, Sally thought she heard the dry corn leaves whisper, "Sally, come dance."

Fatted Squash

" Time to slaughter the fatted squash," said Dad. He placed a huge pumpkin on the newspaper-covered kitchen table.

Maddy and I stood nearby watching Dad stab the orange squash with a butcher knife. There was a hiss, and then the sound of sawing.

"What kind of face do you want on the jack-o'-lantern this year?" Dad asked as he pulled the serrated blade up and down, slicing a rough circle. "Scary, evil, or goofy?"

"Scary!" squealed Maddy.

My sister had always been braver than me.

"Or goofy," I suggested as Dad tugged the top off the pumpkin.

Dad and Maddy rolled their eyes at my suggestion. I knew they wanted an evil-looking jack-o'-lantern.

"We will vote later," said my father.

I already knew I would be outvoted. Our jack-o'-lantern would be the scariest one in the neighborhood. The candle flickering inside the huge orange squash would make it look alive. Once again, I would run past our jack-o'-lantern every time I went in or out of the front door. To be honest, I was surprised candy lured trick-or-treaters past our horrifying pumpkin year after year.

After Dad slashed a web of orange membranes from the pumpkin's lid, he turned the squash over to Maddy and me.

"Scrape out its brains," he said.

As Maddy pulled the fibrous gunk out of the squash with her bare hands, I swear I heard the pumpkin moan.

"Come on, Topher," my sister urged, "grab some of the pumpkin's brains. You should help get it ready for a face, too."

With a sigh, I picked up my spoon. To keep Maddy happy, I scraped at the inside of the pumpkin. The sound of metal tearing at pumpkin flesh caused the hairs on my arms to stand up.

"This really isn't my thing," I said. Gritting my teeth, I spooned another glob of orange-colored scrapings onto the newspapers.

"It is nothing but a vegetable," Dad reminded me.

"Still..." I began.

"You think it has feelings?" Maddy asked.

Then, both my sister and father laughed at me while Dad carved a horrifying grimace into the pumpkin.

"I'm going to spend the night at Uncle Tim's house," I announced. I packed my knapsack for school the next day. Maddy and Dad were still giggling as I walked out the door.

But no one was chuckling in the morning when the police called Uncle Tim and me. Dad and Maddy were dead. Someone had broken into the house. There were no footprints or fingerprints to be found, only smears of mud and drizzled pumpkin juice.

The police said Dad and Maddy had been strangled with pumpkin vines by an unknown assailant. I knew they would never find the culprit. No one ever looked for a murderer in a pumpkin patch.

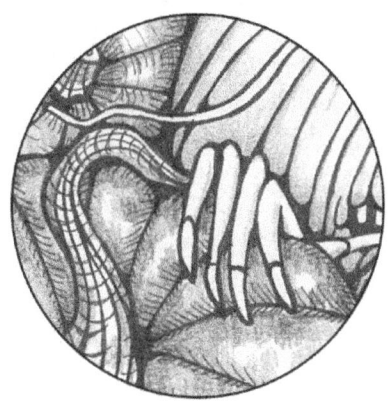

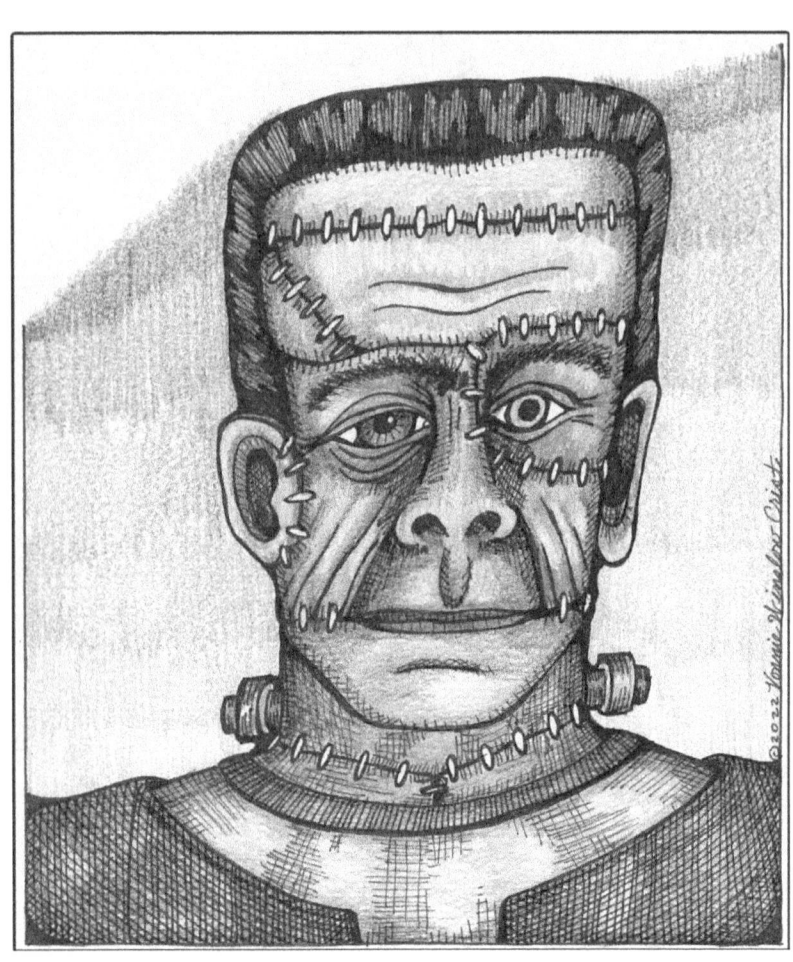

Doctor Frankenstein's Monster

Reconstructed of mismatched parts,
he returned to his beloved.

Terrified, she locked him out.
But he dismantled the door.

Halloween Surprise

Too old to beg for candy, Maddox decided to play a prank. He thought it would be fun to frighten his younger sister and her friends while they were trick-or-treating.

The Halloween moon was nearly full, so Maddox didn't take a flashlight with him. His sister, Adelaide, and her friends, Camie, Tara, Julie, and Liz walked close together. Each girl carried a bag for collecting candy. They talked as they went from house to house.

Careful to remain out of sight, Maddox followed them.

Be patient. Wait until the right moment if you really want to frighten them, he told himself.

Then, he spotted a graveyard the girls would pass on their way to the next group of homes. After hurrying ahead, Maddox climbed the cemetery's wall. He crouched down.

The wind had risen. He noticed the iron cemetery gate squeaked as it pulled against its chains. Maddox glanced around. It was an old graveyard. The graves had sunken. Many of the tombstones were tilted. A few headstones had fallen or been pushed over.

Maybe this isn't such a good idea, Maddox thought. His heart beat faster as the wind rattled the gate's chains once more.

He spotted Adelaide and her friends approaching. *Just a few minutes more*, he told himself. *Then, you can get out of this creepy place.*

But *he* was the one surprised, when rotten hands reached

from the grave beneath his feet. The hands grasped his ankles and pulled him down. He yelled for help, but the wind swallowed his voice.

The last words he heard as the sod closed over his head were, "GOT YOU!"*

*If you are reading this story to friends, grab the shoulder of someone sitting near you when you say this.

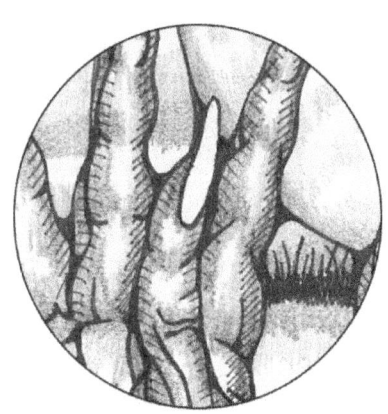

©2022　Vonnie Winslow Crist

Strays

"Is that your cat?" asked Roy.

"No." Holly shook her head.

Holly and Roy studied the sooty feline sitting beside the jack-o'-lantern on Holly's porch.

The stray cat yawned.

"Maybe it's a were-cat." Roy stepped back. "And when we turn our backs, it will change into a blood-sucking monster."

"Don't be silly." Holly bent down and reached for the stray. The black cat sniffed her hand. It bent its head and rubbed against Holly.

"Aw. He likes me." Holly stroked the cat's back. Its back arched up to meet her hand. With a smile on her face, Holly picked up the stray.

"Be careful. It might have rabies," said Roy. He didn't like the look in the stray cat's green eyes.

"There is nothing to worry about," replied Holly. "Listen, the cat is purring."

Roy shook his head and warned, "You had better put that cat down. You never know what sort of mischief might happen on Halloween," Then, he departed for his house.

Later, Roy returned to see if Holly wanted to go trick-or-treating. Holly was nowhere to be found, but beside her jack-o'-lantern were *two* black cats with strange green eyes.

"Holly?" he whispered.

The smaller of the cats stood up and lifted her front paw. She meowed.

Roy thought the meow sounded like the cat was saying, "Help. Help."

Terrified, Roy ran home. He didn't dare look behind to see if the stray cats were following.

Fountain

"Let's go to my house and play," suggested Anna. Katie nodded, then asked her mother, "May I walk to Anna's house?"

"Yes," replied Katie's mother. "Remember to stay on the sidewalk and don't cut through the woods. I will drive over before dinner and pick you up."

"Okay," called Katie as she and her best friend, Anna, skipped out the door.

"If we use the sidewalk, it is more than a mile to my home," said Anna as the friends walked. "If we take a path through the woods, it's much closer."

"But I told my mom—" began Katie.

"She will never know we used a shortcut," said Anna as she veered from the sidewalk.

"Wait!" yelled Katie.

Soon, both girls were strolling down a dirt trail that disappeared into the forest's shadows. They hadn't gone far when they spotted a smaller path leading to a slightly opened iron gate. A metal sign that said FANGTHORN was attached to the stone wall to the right of the gate.

"Cool!" Anna went to the gate, pushed it open, then turned to look at Katie. "Come on. Let's see what Fangthorn stands for."

"I don't think we should," Katie managed to say before Anna walked through the gate and disappeared behind the stone wall.

Afraid to be in the woods alone, Katie ran after her friend.

"Wow!" exclaimed Katie. As soon as she got inside the stone wall, she saw dozens and dozens of overgrown rosebushes lining a stone walkway. The thorny plants were covered in red and pink blooms.

Anna stood a few yards further down the cobblestone path. "I hear water," she said. "Maybe it's a waterfall."

Again, her friend ran ahead. Katie sighed. She had come this far; she might as well see what was making the gurgling noise. She hurried deeper into the brambly woods of Fangthorn. The rambling roses pressed closer. The trees became so thick they cut off most of the sunlight. Soon, the cobblestones were nearly hidden by moss.

All of a sudden, the path widened into a small circular patio. In the center was a large fountain. Anna stood in front of the fountain. On the other side, a hooded figure loomed.

Katie put her hand to her mouth when she saw dozens of snakes crawling around the fountain and swimming in its basins.

"Welcome," hissed the hooded figure. "What is your business with the Guardian of Fangthorn?"

"No business," said Anna. "I saw the open gate and I was curious."

"Hm." The hooded figure, whom Katie assumed was the Guardian, turned its head to look at her. "And you?"

"I was worried about my friend. Then, when I saw your beautiful roses, I wanted to see more of the garden." She paused and took a deep breath. "I am sorry we trespassed. We would be happy to leave."

"Not so fast," whispered the Guardian. "Trespassers must prove their worth."

Though Katie's legs felt like jelly, she took several steps forward. Putting her arm around Anna, she asked, "What must we do?"

The Guardian smiled a terrible smile. "You each must scoop a handful of water, then drink it. The snakes are not venomous, but they might bite you, nevertheless. Then, you may depart."

Anna glanced in Katie's direction. Katie saw she was frightened.

"Together," said Katie as she took her friend's hand.

Together the girls plunged their hands into the water. Both screamed as the snakes crawled across their skin. Undeterred, they cupped their hands, brought some water to their mouths, and drank it.

The Guardian raised an arm and pointed toward the gate. Katie shivered when she saw the creature's hand was covered in scales.

"Leave, but know from this day forward, the roses, snakes, and I will watch you. One day, I will collect payment for your curiosity and mouthful of water."

Katie heard rustling in the nearby rosebushes. A green-skinned face peeked out. Within seconds, more than twenty other goblins popped their heads up from the roses.

"Run!" shouted Katie as she grabbed Anna's hand.

The girls raced up the cobblestone walkway, through the gate, and back to the sidewalk. Still running, they headed to Anna's house by way of the sidewalk. When they finally arrived at the white, two-story home where Anna and her parents lived, they flopped on the porch.

"That was close," said Anna. Returning to her usually brave and reckless self, she laughed. "I don't think we will take that shortcut again."

"No," replied Katie. "At least not until the Guardian summons us."

She traced a snake-shaped birthmark that had appeared on the wrist of the hand she'd dipped in the fountain at Fangthorn.

Anna gasped. A snake-shaped birthmark had also appeared on her wrist.

Slowly, the blossoms on the rosebushes on either side of the porch turned to face the girls. Then, Katie pointed at a garter snake curled up in the corner of the porch.

Finally, a snaky voice hissed from the shadows, "See you soon."

Wildwood Church

Indira stared at a dilapidated church nestled in the woods. "I don't think we should go inside," she said.

"I bet it is abandoned." Duff opened the door. "Come on. Let's explore it."

"Let's not," replied Indira.

"I am going inside, whether you come or not," said Duff.

Indira didn't want her friend to go inside alone. She was afraid he might fall through the floorboards and hurt himself. "I will go in for a few minutes, but we are not going to spend much time in there," she said.

"Great!" Duff stepped inside.

Indira followed.

As soon as they walked into the church, Duff coughed. "What reeks?" he asked.

"It smells like something is dead," answered Indira. "We should leave."

Duff ignored her. He pushed aside some debris. "Geeze, it stinks even worse."

"Quiet, Duff." Indira put her hand on his shoulder. "I hear scraping. Maybe someone is trapped in here."

"Nope," said Duff as he pointed at two bodies sprawled in the corner of the room. "I think they are beyond rescue."

Indira gasped. "Look at their faces. Something has gnawed on them."

Hearing a groan, Indira and Duff glanced left.

An animated corpse stood there. It was gnashing its teeth

and growling.

They fled from the church. Running as fast as their legs could carry them, Indira and Duff raced past headstones and open graves. Breathing heavily, they rushed down the forest path that led to their homes.

Indira wondered if the zombie following them was slow or fast moving, because her legs were tiring. Of course, Indira knew she only had to run a little bit faster than Duff. The zombie would be satisfied once it caught the slowest runner and started to eat.

She glanced at Duff. The fear in his eyes told her he was thinking the same thing.

And then, Indira stumbled.

Wren Boys

"**Y**ou need to hunt and murder a wren," said Sean as he buttoned his raggedy jacket.

His brothers, Will and Joe, stood behind him, nodding masked faces.

"It is the only way we can get people to give us money," said Will. He pulled his torn sweatshirt's hood up so the string used to tie his mask in place was hidden.

"What?" Davy had been unsure about being a Wren Boy since his schoolmates proposed it after Christmas church service. "I am not killing a bird."

"We need a dead wren to tie to a stick and decorate with ribbons," explained Will. "Sean, Joe, and I already collected ribbon from our Christmas presents and hung it on this mop handle." He shook the green, ribboned pole he held. "All that is missing is the bird. So that is *your* contribution to our Wren Boys parade."

"Four kids is hardly a parade," replied Davy. He had known from the get-go the O'Brien boys were trouble. Why he had agreed to participate in their moneymaking scheme he didn't know.

Yes you do, he told himself. *You are an unpopular bookworm. You wanted Sean, Will, and Joe to like you.*

Joe beating on a toy drum interrupted Davy's thoughts.

"The money people give us is for the wren's burial expenses." Sean wiped his nose with the back of his left glove. "Of course, we are keeping the money. Then, we are going to toss the bird's body into Asher's Woods."

"When I said I would come, I thought we were just walking around the neighborhood dressed like beggars. I thought we would be singing songs and getting punch and cookies. You know, like carolers." The thought of killing an animal, even a wren, made Davy's stomach knot up.

"Chicken?" asked Sean in a tone of voice that declared he believed Davy *was* lily-livered.

"No..." Davy tried to think of an excuse.

"He's a scaredy cat," mocked Will as he tried to scratch his cheek under his mask without taking it off.

"Not true," replied Davy. "I just didn't want us to get some disease because we touched a wren. A fake bird from my family's Christmas tree would be better. We can sprinkle red paint on it, so it looks like it was murdered."

Will and Joe nodded.

Davy knew they were the weaker of the trio. Sean would decide.

"Loser," scoffed Sean. "We will kill our own wren. And *we* will keep all the money. You are officially uninvited to be a Wren Boy. So don't follow us into Asher's Woods."

"Be careful," warned Davy as a chilly wind caused the wren pole's ribbons to flutter. "I heard there is a guardian spirit living in those woods. It might not like you killing a wren."

"Weirdo," shouted Sean over his shoulder.

Still standing on his porch, Davy saw the shadow of a buzzard move across the snow in front of the O'Brien brothers as they marched to the beat of Joe's drum toward Asher's Woods. He shivered.

***

That evening, Davy listened as the television newscaster reported: "The bodies of three local boys were discovered in Asher's Woods late today. Apparently attacked by animals, the authorities are awaiting the coroner's report before confirming the exact nature of their deaths. Anyone with information should call..."

Davy didn't listen to the rest of the report. Instead, he looked out the frosted windowpane at the woods across the street. He half expected to see a guardian spirit with a singing wren perched on its shoulder and a wicked blade in its hand, looking back.

But all he saw were the shadows of tree branches clawing the snow.

Mitten Tree

In December, when she moved into a charming house in a
picket-fence neighborhood, Drucilla Darkwander decided
to set aside her witchy ways. Only one day passed before
her neighbors, the Testermans, tested her resolve.

"Sorry about your flowers," said one of the girls on day
two.

Drucilla glanced at her garden. A group of Testermans
had smashed her herbs while retrieving their soccer ball.

"Hm," replied Drucilla Darkwander.

"Too bad about your fence," called a Testerman boy on day
three after he crashed his minibike into the pickets of her
newly-painted fence.

"Hm," murmured Drucilla.

On day four, after she'd shooed her neighbor's dogs away
from her roses, a spell popped into Drucilla's mind. She
ignored it until Lila, the matriarch of the ill-mannered
Testerman clan, quipped, "Dogs will be dogs."

Drucilla's eyes narrowed as Mrs. Testerman dragged the
baying hounds home.

"I must do something," she whispered. The magic in her
veins burned hotter than a Christmas pudding. "But what?"
she said to her cat.

Shadow tugged a yarn ball from her knitting bag. He
mewed.

"Mittens!" exclaimed the witchy woman who had decided
to embrace magic one last time.

Drucilla searched her pattern drawer. She located directions for mittens. Then, she grabbed worsted-weight yarn from her stash and picked up a pair of needles. Still angry with her neighbors, she cast on twenty-three stitches. Next, she knitted four rows of stockinette stitch for the cuff.

"Time for hair," she told Shadow. The cat had positioned himself on the windowsill where he could monitor the Testermans, balls of yarn, and Drucilla.

She retrieved her hairbrush from the bathroom. "Plenty of hair for our needs."

Shadow groomed his shoulder.

Placing a strand of her hair alongside the yarn, Drucilla knitted it into the remainder of the cuff while chanting a binding spell. Once her hair was woven tightly into the fabric of the mitten, she continued knitting until the mitten was completed. Knowing she could complete more mittens with another pinch of magic, Drucilla spoke a speed spell. She hummed as her needles clicked in double-time.

Throughout December, the Testermans annoyed Drucilla. They trespassed, damaged her gardens, kicked balls against the side of her house, and allowed their dogs to dig in her lawn. *If* they apologized, Drucilla acknowledged them with a forced smile.

For days, as she chanted binding spells, Drucilla knitted mittens in various sizes and colors. Only she and Shadow knew each mitten had one of her hairs stitched into it. On Christmas Eve, Shadow purred as she tied the pairs together with red-as-blood yarn and loaded them into a bag.

"Our problems are nearly solved," she told her cat when she stepped outside.

Shadow jumped to his favorite spot. He peered through the windowpane.

Quick as a needle poke, Drucilla tied the mittens onto a fir tree located on her front lawn. Next, she walked to the Testermans' front door. She knocked three times.

"Ms. Darkwander," said Lila Testerman as she opened the door.

"I've made mittens for your family. Won't you all come

over and pick a pair from my mitten tree," said Drucilla. She smiled slyly.

"How nice!" exclaimed Lila before shouting for her brood.

Like a cackle of hyenas, the Testermans raced to the evergreen. They argued over who got which mittens. Still squabbling, they stripped the mitten tree. Finally, the Testermans clamored back to their house with nary a "thank you" from the bunch.

Chuckling, Drucilla Darkwander walked inside her cozy house. Now that *they* possessed enchanted mittens with a part of her woven into them, Drucilla could possess the Testermans.

She picked up her knitting needles. She wondered what sharp things the wretched Testermans would receive for Christmas. Drucilla smiled as she considered exactly what, or who, she would tell them to stab in the morning.

Shadow tilted his head, twitched his whiskers, and patted Drucilla's wrinkled hand with his velvety paw.

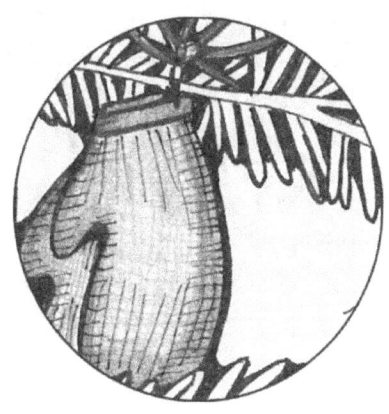

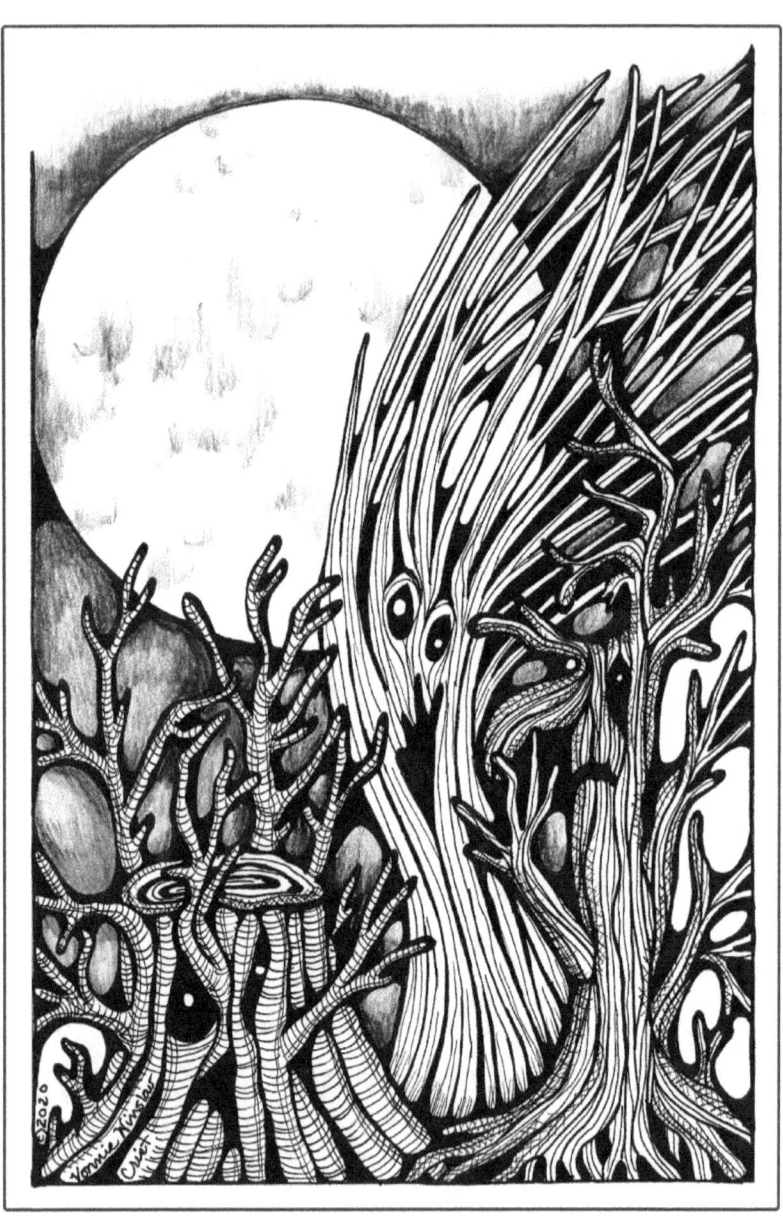

Ogerhunches

Brendan kicked one of CeCe's wooden blocks. He was stuck watching his little sister while their grandmother made supper.

"Come on, CeCe," he said as he opened the screen door. "Let's take a walk."

"Okay," she replied. The six-year-old grabbed a teddy bear and skipped out the door. "But I lead the way," she added.

"Yeah, yeah." Brendan knew it was no use arguing with her. She would just start to cry. Then, Granny would remind him he was eleven, and he should just let CeCe *think* she was the boss.

"It is a full moon tonight," Granny called after them. "Make sure to put nails in your pockets. And watch out for ogerhunches."

Brendan sighed. Again, it was easier to slip a nail into CeCe's and his pockets rather than argue. Like her grandmother before her, Granny still believed in fairies and goblins. If Brendan refused, he would find himself in the house playing dolls with CeCe.

"We both got a nail," Brendan shouted as his sister and he raced towards the woods.

"Last one to the fort is a rotten egg," yelled CeCe. She sprinted down the path.

Brendan ran fast enough to catch up to her but didn't run past his sister. If he made the effort, the two of them could get along until supper. Mom would be arriving home from work at suppertime. Then, he would be off babysitting duty and able to play a video game.

Finally, they reached the tree fort. He watched CeCe climb the ladder up to the wooden structure to make sure she didn't slip and fall.

She really does well for her age, he thought. Though he would never tell her that. If he did, she would want to tag along even more when he went places with his friends.

Once CeCe was safely up, Brendan followed.

They hadn't been in the fort for a minute, when CeCe said, "Tell me a story, Brendan."

"Sure." He grinned, thinking of Granny's warning. Then, he began the story, "Once upon a time, there were two children playing in the woods."

"Just like us." CeCe laughed.

"Yes," said Brendan. Knowing he would probably scare CeCe, he continued his tale nonetheless. "They were naughty children. They had not listened to their grandmother. They didn't put an iron nail in their pockets to keep away the ogerhunch goblins."

CeCe's eyes widen. She held her teddy bear against her chest.

"When they were deep in the forest, they heard the ogerhunches moving closer," said Brendan.

"What do ogerhunches look like?" asked CeCe in a small voice.

"They are nasty goblins that look like small dead trees, fallen branches, old logs, and piles of leaves," he answered. Repeating one of Granny's descriptions, he added, "When they come for you, they come in groups. The ogerhunches knock you down to the ground with their branch-like arms. Next, they suck out all your blood and guts with their root toes. It is a terrible death."

"I am ready to go back to Granny's house," said CeCe before popping her thumb into her mouth.

"Shoot!" Brendan knew he had gone too far. He had really frightened his sister. "But we don't have to worry, CeCe, because we have our nails." He reached into his pocket and showed her his nail.

CeCe felt around in her pocket. "I have lost mine," she cried. "Now, the ogerhunch goblins can get me."

"Don't worry," he assured his sister. "If any ogerhunches show up, I'll carry you."

"Okay, Brendan," said CeCe, "but I still want to go back."

"Fine, I will climb down first." After reaching the ground, Brendan waited for his sister at the bottom of the ladder. As he waited, he noticed some movement in the forest undergrowth.

It's just your imagination, he told himself.

As soon as CeCe stepped on the leaves at the foot of the tree fort oak, one of the nearby saplings crept closer. Next, a pile of pine needles and broken twigs beside them rose in the shape of man.

"Ogerhunches," gasped his sister as she pointed to a rotten log that had just sat up. The upright log opened a gaping mouth in its bark.

"Run," urged Brendan. "I am right behind you."

They sprinted toward Granny's house, but on either side of the path, more ogerhunches pushed closer. The foul woodland goblins waved their branch arms and gnashed their wooden teeth.

Suddenly, one of the ogerhunches knocked CeCe to the ground. As Brendan reached for her, he saw dozens of rootlets grabbing her legs and arms. He heard sucking sounds as the roots touched her skin.

"No," he screamed. He pushed away the ogerhunches' roots and picked up his sister. Though small for her age, CeCe was still a lot for Brendan to carry. He stumbled as he did his best to keep his sister from touching the forest floor. Despite his efforts, the ogerhunches were determined to have CeCe for their dinner.

As one of the ogerhunch goblins swung its branches at his head, Brendan ducked. But by ducking, he lost his balance and tumbled to the ground. Worst of all, he dropped CeCe as he fell.

A swarm of ogerhunches came at them from all sides.

Brendan held his sister close and prayed his nail would protect them both. But he doubted it would. Its power would be split in half. Without more protection, they would both be dinner for the goblins.

He had given up hope of surviving when he heard his grandmother's voice calling, "Get back or I will roast you."

Brendan saw Granny carrying a flaming torch coming toward CeCe and him. She wore jangling bells, red ribbons, and a necklace of iron nails. He suspected she also carried a four-leafed clover or two to keep fairy folk away.

"Get up," she shouted, "and come to me."

Brendan stood. He picked up his sobbing sister and stumbled to Granny.

Meanwhile, his grandmother swung her torch around. She shouted at the ogerhunches, "I will set you afire, goblins, if you hurt my grandbabies."

A quick glance at the faces of the ogerhunches showed terror in their beady black eyes. *Fire*, he thought, *must be what ogerhunches fear the most.* Which made sense if they were truly part of the forest.

When CeCe and Brendan were finally beside their grandmother, Granny slipped her nail necklace over his sister's head. "Now, let's go home for supper," she said.

The three of them hurried back to Granny's yard. Before he went into the house, Brendan glanced back at the woods. Standing like a row of wooden nightmares on the other side of the iron fence surrounding his grandmother's lawn were dozens of ogerhunches. Several of them pointed their twig-like fingers at him. With an ugly expression on their faces, they opened and shut their wooden mouths.

Brendan grabbed an extra nail from the bucket on the porch and slipped it into his pocket before he went inside. He didn't think he would go anywhere without protection from fairies and goblins again. Full moon or not.

On a Quiet Road

Her ghostly form moves slowly,
as she abandons her grave,
departs the cemetery,
and walks beside the highway.

Lonely, she looks for company.
One car, then two trucks pass by,
but no one notices Sara
silently standing there.

When the next car approaches,
Sara steps into the road.
The driver stops and asks
if she would like a ride.

"Yes," she whispers with a smile
as she climbs into the front seat.
"You should not be out here alone,"
warns the driver as he glances at Sara.

"Neither should you," she answers
before causing his car to crash into a tree.
A few seconds later, Sara and the driver
float back to the graveyard.

She is no longer lonely.

Night Raven

"Go to sleep, Gretchen," said Papa as he turned to leave her bedroom.

"I can't sleep," said Gretchen. Holding a patchwork quilt's edge under her chin, she sat up. "I hear storm gusts bending the trees. What if it is the Night Raven searching for children?"

"Don't believe the foolish stories your grandfather tells. There is no *Nachtkrapp*, no Night Raven wandering the world in a whirlwind looking to snatch children."

"But Granddad said..."

"Enough. Go to sleep." Papa pulled the door closed. Gretchen heard his footsteps as he walked down the hall.

As soon as her father's footsteps stopped, Gretchen heard tapping on her window.

"It is nothing but a branch wagging in the wind," she told the stuffed bear tucked beneath the covers by her side.

She heard the window latch jiggle.

"I wish the wind would stop playing with the lock," said Gretchen to her bear.

The bear said nothing. It only stared at her with its button eyes.

She heard the window slam against the wall and felt a cold draft.

"Papa!"

"Papa is not coming," said a deep voice. "He doesn't believe."

Gretchen kept her eyes focused on her bear. She knew to gaze into the empty eye sockets of the *Nachtkrapp* meant death. She whispered, "But I believe, Night Raven. So please don't carry me away and devour me."

The man-sized creature ruffled its feathers, clacked its beak, and tiptoed on clawed feet across the room to stand by Gretchen's bed.

The Night Raven bent down and whispered, "All children become believers when they gaze at my tattered wings and fall ill. All parents believe after I have abducted their little ones."

Smelling death on the monster's breath as it leaned over her, Gretchen asked, "Why not be the *Guter Nachtkrapp* tonight?"

"The Good Night Raven?" The creature chuckled. "I suppose I could. You know my true names and have been most polite." He tapped one of his claws on the floor of Gretchen's bedroom. Next, he clicked his sharp beak. Finally, he spoke. "Of course, if we become friends, I will visit you often."

The thought of the Night Raven visiting her again and again terrified Gretchen. But she knew she had no choice. So she snuggled beneath her covers, held tight to her teddy bear, and said, "Deal."

The Night Raven brushed her brow with his wing feathers. He sat on the edge of her bed. Then, in a voice like the moan of winter air rushing through a graveyard, he sang a lullaby to Gretchen until she fell asleep.

After brushing her brow once more, the Night Raven stood. He strode across the room, slipped out the window, and wandered into the night. There were still bad children to be snatched.

From the Author

Since a young age, I have listened to, read, and imagined scary tales. All the stories, poems, and illustrations in *Shivers, Scares and Goosebumps* came from my imagination. Some of them began with folklore, superstitions, and urban legends. You can check *Notes* to read more about the beginning place for the stories and poems.

I hope you enjoy my spooky words and drawings.

– Vonnie Winslow Crist

Notes

1. Mudpuppy: Though mudpuppies (*Necturus maculosus*) are carnivorous, they do not attack people (except in my imagination).
2. Clean Your Room: Monsters and other creatures hiding under the bed are urban legends.
3 Lunar Phase: Werewolves (people who can change into wolves) are shapeshifters from folklore. In most werewolf legends, moonlight is needed for a person to change into a wolf.
4. Ghost Pack: Ghosts and other undead creatures returning to settle their affairs are folklore. There are lots of urban legends built on this folklore.
5. Under Toad: When I was a child, I misunderstood the word *undertow*. I imagined a terrible toad waiting to drag me below the ocean's waves.
6. Saying Goodbye: Ghosts visiting to say farewell to loved ones is an urban legend.
7. Trophies: Ghosts or other undead creatures returning for revenge is a common folk belief. Many urban legends are built on this folklore.
8. Vampire: These former humans who take the life force from others to live forever are a part of folklore. Often, the vampire drinks the blood of their victims. One of the most famous vampire stories is told in Bram Stoker's 1897 book, *Dracula*.
9. One Easter: This story is based on folkways from Finland. Dressing up like witches and chasing away evil spirits, blessing homes with willow twigs, and receiving candy have merged to make Easter a fun holiday.
10. Vultures: Turkey vultures (*Cathartes aura*) eat carrion. They prefer recently dead animals. Occasionally, they will kill prey that is much smaller than humans.

11. Visiting: Seeing dead relatives when you go to a graveyard is a folk belief which has grown into different urban legends.

12: Tooth Fairy: The Tooth Fairy is a folklore and fairytale being. When a baby tooth falls out, the child puts the tooth under their pillow. The Tooth Fairy visits the child at night. She takes the tooth and leaves behind money.

13. Last Farm: Lots of haunted house urban legends began with the folk belief that ghosts haunt their former home.

14. Whistle Past: Kalma is the Finnish goddess of death and decay. She rides a cloud of stench. "Whistle past the graveyard" is a saying that means a person is trying to act brave even when they are frightened.

15. Aliens: Hairless, big-eyed creatures from outer space visiting and sometimes abducting humans is an urban legend.

16. Scarecrow Dance: A scarecrow that comes to life is an urban legend.

17. Fatted Squash: When we carved our pumpkin each Halloween, I told my children it was time to "slaughter the fatted squash." In this story, I consider the pumpkin's point of view!

18. Doctor Frankenstein's Monster: This poem is a nod to Mary Shelley and her 1818 book, *Frankenstein, or the Modern Prometheus*.

19. Halloween Surprise: When I was a teen, I hid in a graveyard waiting to scare my friends. The ground was so soft, it felt like someone was trying to pull me into a grave.

20. Strays: Werewolves aren't the only shape changers in folklore. I decided to write about a werecat!

21. Fountain: Many folk and fairy tales feature children wandering into the dangerous, unpredictable forest. Often, the children disobey their parents and leave the path.

22. Wildwood Church: In some cultures, zombies are dead people who come back to life and prey on the living. They have become part of our urban legends.

23. Wren Boys: On December 26, an Irish, Welsh, and English custom based on folklore is for the Wren Boys to kill

a wren, dress up, then parade around town asking for money.

24. Mitten Tree: There are many superstitions concerning human hair. One is if someone finds some of your hair, they can put a hex on you. Another is if you wear an item of clothing with another person's hair woven into it, that person will have control over you.

25. Ogerhunches: One of the amazing words I found in Jeffery Kacirk's *The Word Museum* was *ogerhunch*. According to Kacirk, an *ogerhunch* is "any frightful or loathsome creature..." It is a term from Scottish folklore. I decided to make my ogerhunches goblins that looked like forest debris.

26. On a Quiet Road: Ghosts beckoning drivers to their deaths is an often-shared urban legend.

27. Night Raven: The *Nachtkrapp* or Night Raven is a creature originally from German folklore. It was used to scare naughty children into behaving. The *Guter Nachtkrapp* is the good version of the Night Raven. It will sing children to sleep rather than kidnap them when it enters their rooms at night. Many other European countries have a Night Raven in their folklore as well.

Acknowledgements

Thanks to Dawn Schiavone Crist for her friendship and invaluable critiquing, Andrea Thomas for insightful editing, and Dark Owl Publishing for taking a chance on a book of shivery, scary, goosebump-inducing stories. Thank you to my friends and family for supporting my creative endeavors and patiently listening to me spin fantastical tales. Lastly, a special thanks to Ernie for always being there.

About the Author

Born in the Year of the Dragon, Vonnie Winslow Crist, MS Professional Writing, has had a lifelong interest in reading, writing, art, science fiction, myth, fairytales, folklore, and legends. An award-winning author and illustrator, she is a member of the Science Fiction & Fantasy Writers of America, Horror Writers Association, Society of Children's Book Writers & Illustrators, and National League of American Pen Women. Her speculative stories and poems have been published in Italy, Spain, Finland, Germany, India, Australia, Japan, Canada, the UK, and USA.

A cloverhand who believes the world is still filled with mystery, magic, and miracles, she loves to hear from readers at conventions, conferences, and online. Visit her website at http://vonniewinslowcrist.com or connect with her on Facebook at facebook.com/WriterVonnieWinslowCrist.

A little boy gets lost in the big woods.
His parents are so worried and are trying to find him.
He gets found, but by the most unlikely of creatures,
and she becomes the most unlikely of friends.

ANNETTE
A Big, Hairy Mom

Written and Illustrated by
JOHN S. MCFARLAND

Available in paperback and on Kindle
October 15, 2022
from Dark Owl Publishing, LLC
www.darkowlpublishing.com

Grayson North can't catch a break.

That is,
until he inherits a silvery key with copper bands.
He suddenly gains wintery superpowers
and a world of epic responsibility.
He must protect the City of Chicago from the firey
extra-dimensional monsters known as Sulfurians.

But can he master his powers and uncover
the Sulfurians' plans to bring back the
Great Chicago Fire before it's too late?

COME TO DARK OWL'S WEBSITE
AND VISIT

The
Young Readers
Bookstore

OUR CURRENT AND UPCOMING YOUNG
READER BOOKS ARE FOR A VARIETY OF
READING LEVELS!

**And we rate the appropriateness of all
Dark Owl's books on our YR Bookstore page.**

Visit us at
www.darkowlpublishing.com/the-yr-bookstore

And we're on

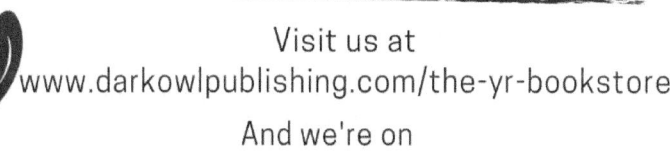